FINGAL

B

Based on **Ossian**,

A Molendinar Production

Fingal is copyright © 2021 John McShane

The moral right of the author has been asserted.

All rights reserved.

No part of this book may be reproduced or transmitted in any form or by any electronic or mechanical means, including photocopying, recording, or by any information and retrieval system, without the written permission of the author, except where permitted by law.

Cover painting by Alex Ronald

Published by Molendinar Productions, Caird Drive, Glasgow

Dedicated to:
Ronnie Renton
Jane Quigley
Pat Mills
John Wagner

And in memory of:
Derick Thomson
Alexander Scott
George Jackson
Michael Ferguson

"John McShane's modernised abridgement of Fingal has real freshness and verve. It is an excellent introduction to the phenomenon of James Macpherson's Ossianic writings which were to become a major stimulus to European Romanticism."
RONNIE RENTON

"An extremely enjoyable dip into Celtic lore that makes me want to explore it in more depth."
JOHN WAGNER

Contents

1. Introduction
2. Fingal
3. Characters, Gods, Places
4. Macpherson's Tales of Ossian
5. The Dr Johnson Controversy
6. Derick Thomson and the Gaelic Sources
7. Macpherson's Method of Composition
8. The Story of the Douai MS
9. The History behind the Myth
10. The Scots Musical Museum – Ossian in Song
11. Chronology of the Works of Ossian
12. Epilogue
13. Bibliography

Introduction

"A great poet is greater than any king. His songs are mightier than my sceptre; for he has near ripped the heart from my breast when he chose to sing for me. I shall die and be forgotten, but Rinaldo's songs will live forever."
Robert E. Howard, The Phoenix on the Sword, 1st story of Conan, Weird Tales, 1932

"Alors, mettrais-tu tes genouillères en vente,
Ô vieillard? Pèlerin sacré! Barde d'Armor!"
Arthur Rimbaud, L'Homme juste, 1871; the Bard is Ossian

James Macpherson's collections of the works of Ossian, which include the story of Fingal, were not just a hit, they were arguably the greatest hit of the 18th century. These poems and songs which Macpherson claimed to have translated from ancient Gaelic originals set the world on fire. In his 1818 essay, On Poetry in General, William Hazlitt leaves us in no doubt how important he thinks these works are:

> "I shall conclude this general account with some remarks on four of the principal works of poetry in the world, at different periods of history – Homer, the Bible, Dante, and let me add, **Ossian**." [My emphasis – note, famous not just in Badenoch where Macpherson was born, nor just in Scotland, but in the world and taking in all the world's literature.]

Surely Hazlitt is exaggerating?

Over in America, Walt Whitman didn't think this was in any way an exaggeration, for he also classed Ossian with the Bible. He thought Red Jacket, an Iroquois orator, was "like one of Ossian's ghosts".

One of Germany's most famous writers, Johann Wolfgang von Goethe (a very influential man who among other things invented a colour wheel and encouraged the creation of the graphic novel) has one of his characters proclaim, in The Sorrows of Young Werther: "Ossian has superseded Homer in my heart.

And later in the same novel, his characters decide "that their fate was pictured in the misfortunes of Ossian's heroes, they felt this together and their tears redoubled".

Robert Burns included two songs of Ossian in the collection The Scots Musical Museum and the tunes could have been taken from the singing of Macpherson himself, although this cannot be proved. Another Robert, Robert E. Howard was inspired by the Scottish legends to write King Kull, Bran Mak Morn, and Conan.

Beethoven, Brahms, Haydn, and Schubert all wrote music inspired by Ossian. And, of course, there are: The Hebrides Overture, or Fingal's Cave and Symphony No 3 (Scotch) in A Minor, both by Mendelssohn.

I could go on and tell you that Thomas Jefferson also said Ossian was better than Homer, or that Napoleon carried a copy of Ossian with him on all his campaigns and had a bust of Ossian painted on the roof of the Malmaison, or that Ezra Pound stated unequivocally, "The Romantic awakening dates from the production of Ossian".

So much for the popularity among famous people, but what of actual sales? Between 1760 and 1773, Macpherson published several editions of Ossianic poetry. George Chambers remarked on 17th July 1805: "Except the Bible and Shakespeare, there is not any book that sells better than Ossian."

So, what happened? Why have you probably not read it before? Why, indeed, have you possibly not even heard of it?

There are two main problems:

Macpherson is not a very good writer; he often inserts irrelevant episodes which ruin the tension when it should be built up. He was in need of a good editor.

Doctor Samuel Johnson said that the entire enterprise was a hoax, a fraud, not at all based on ancient Gaelic originals.

For those readers who wish to learn more about how the Tales of Ossian were composed and want to know if Dr Johnson's accusations which are repeated unchallenged to this day have any validity, I have addressed all the major issues after my edited version of the most important of these tales, Fingal. I have edited out all the needless asides and updated the language. I have endeavoured to get back to the spirit of the original tale, which Macpherson's style obscures. One device I have added are the days of the week. No gods are mentioned in Fingal; in some of the tales there are references to the Norse legends, since they belong to the Scandinavians with whom the Celts had more contact than with the Roman forces beyond the Wall. Indeed, we still use these Norse names for our days of the week.

Fingal is indeed a tale worth telling. Enjoy.

Fingal

Týr's Day

Autumn. Over 1700 years ago. Ulster.

Mighty Cuchullain, guardian of young King Cormac of Erin who was still in his minority, sat under an aspen tree outside the walls of the castle of Tura. His spear lay propped up against the castle wall while his enormous shield, skilfully decorated by the best Celtic craftsmen, lay beside him on the grass. His hand rested on Luath, his faithful, swift-footed dog.

Cuchullain's thoughts were on the last battle he had won. He had slain great Carbar against all odds. He accepted that, had he lost against Carbar, he would have lost also his fame and would have had to retire from battle. But it had turned out well. The poets were proclaiming Cuchullain a renowned invincible warrior and he was inclined to believe them.

His thoughts were interrupted by the sight of Moran, son of Fithil, riding swiftly towards him. Moran was one of the scouts he had sent to the coast to get news of the rumoured invasion of Ulster by the Norseman Swaran, King of Lochlin, that kingdom which ruled Innistore.

"Mighty Cuchullain," said the scout after dismounting and approaching his chief, "I have seen Swaran and some of his fleet of ships. So many are they, I could not see the last of them."

Cuchullain looked up calmly with his clear blue eyes. "Moran, why are you trembling, son of Fithil? Your fears increase the threat. Are you certain these are not the ships of Fingal, King of the Lonely Hills?"

"I saw the King of Lochlin himself," said Moran. "He is tall as a rock of ice. His spear is like yon fir tree. His shield as big as the full moon. He was at the prow of the very first ship and was the first to leave it and sit on a rock on the shore.

"I addressed him directly: 'Many, mighty chieftain, are our brave warriors. In our tongue we call you Garbh, the Giant Man, but many powerful men dwell within Tura's walls.

"He answered me unafraid: 'Who in this land is like me? No hero can stand in my presence. They fall to earth beneath my hand. None can come near Swaran in battle but Fingal, King of the Stormy Hills. Once we two wrestled on the heath of Malmor and our heels upended the trees. Rocks fell from their place. Rivulets, changing their course, fled murmuring from our strife. Three days we fought while so-called heroes stood at a distance and trembled. Fingal has been heard to say that on the fourth day the King of the Ocean fell, but Swaran knows the truth. Let dark Cuchullain yield to him who is as strong as the storms of Malmor.'"

To this tale, blue-eyed Cuchullain replied: "No! I will yield to no man. Dark Cuchullain will be either great or dead. Go, son of Fithil, and take with you my spear. Strike the shield of my grandfather Cabait which hangs at Tura's gate. Its sound is not the sound of peace. My heroes shall hear it wherever they are and will know I summon them to a counsel of war."

Moran took proud Cuchullain's spear and struck the shield embossed with intricate designs. The sound echoed through all the hills and rocks. It spread through the woods and startled the deer beside the lake.

The battle rage came at once on the warriors. Connal of the bloody spear headed at once to the castle. Fair haired Crugal's chest was beating in anticipation of action. Favi's son turned his eyes from the beautiful deer. "The war shield sounds," said Ronnar. "Cuchullain's spear calls us," said Lugar.

The chiefs assembled, each one thinking of their pride in former battles, their characters forged from victory. Their eyes are like flames of fire, rolling in search of their land's foes. Their mighty hands are on their swords, whose blades become lightning in the reflected sun.

Like streams from the mountain pour these warriors as each rush roaring from the hills. Bright are the chieftains in their fathers' armour. Gloomy and dark, the other heroes follow them like a gathering of dark clouds before the storm. And all around, their faithful dogs are barking.

Cuchullain greeted them. "Hail, ye sons of the narrow vales. Hail, ye hunters of the deer. Another sport is drawing near like the waves that crash on the shore. Shall we fight for our land, ye sons of war? Or yield Innisfail to Lochlin? Connal, first of men, breaker of the shields, you have fought before with Lochlin. Will you once again take up your father's shield?"

Connal was calm when he replied. "Cuchullain, you know well my spear is keen. It delights to shine in battle and to mix with the blood of thousands. But, although my hand is bent on war, my heart prefers to keep the peace of Erin. Swaran's masts are as numerous as reeds in a lake. Many are his warriors. So, Connal is for peace."

Calmar, son of Matha, gazed wide-eyed at Connal. "Fly, thou chief of peace! Fly to your silent hills where the spear of battle never shone. Go, you, and chase the dark-brown deer. Use your arrows only to bring down the bounding roes. But you, Cuchullain of the piercing blue eyes, use them to see clearly. You are the ruler of wars. Let us scatter the forces of Lochlin and demolish the ranks of their pride. Let none of their vessels again pass their islands in the north."

Connal paused before he replied. "Never before, son of Matha, did I flee. Swiftly I joined my friends in battle, though small is my fame. I was always there when the battle was won. But hear me, Cuchullain. King Cormac's throne is ancient.

Offer half the land and some riches in exchange for peace. Perhaps then, Fingal will come. Or, if you choose war, great chieftain, I will lift my sword and spear. Then my joy will be in the midst of thousands and my soul shall brighten in the gloom of the fight."

Once again Cuchullain spoke to his assembled warriors. "To me, pleasant is the noise of arms, as pleasant as the thunder before the showers of Spring. But where are the friends who once accompanied me into battle? Where is Cathbat? Four great stones surround his grave. And Duchomar? My own hands have laid him to rest. And both dead for love of Morna. But enough!

> "Fetch me my chariot, attach to it my great horses, load it with my spears."

> Thus Cuchullain led into battle his fierce, vast crowd of warriors, all sons of Erin.

> On the shore, the sons of Lochlin heard the approaching thunder. Swaran took up his shield and summoned Arno's son. "Climb yon hill and view the dark face of the heath."

> The son of Arno, trembling, climbed. He was swift to return, his heart pounding in his chest, his words faltering, broken, slow. "Great chieftain, Lord of the Ocean, Cuchullain's chariot comes swiftly followed by great hordes of men. Shall we retreat, my Lord?"

> "Never!" shouted Swaran. "When have I ever fled from battle? Were Fingal himself to lead those men I would not yield."

> He turned to address his fellow countrymen. "Rise to the battle, my thousands. Gather around your King. You are strong as the rocks of Lochlin. Cuchullain falls this day!"

> Battle cries rose from both sides, deafening was the noise. The shore rang with the clash of steel on steel. Many strong

helmets were cleft from mighty blows. The ground turned red with a sea of blood. The sky darkened with the flight of arrows.

Many heroes fell that day. Many widows were left behind.

Cuchullain's sword descended like the mightiest lightning, destroying all in its path. His steed Dusronnal snorted over the bodies of heroes. And Sifadda bathed his hoof in the blood of warriors.

On Innistore, Trenar's grey dogs began to howl and they saw his passing ghost. His bow will never again be strung. His spouse will embrace him no more.

Night descended, concealing the heroes in her clouds. As swiftly as the battle commenced, so swiftly did it end.

Back at Tura, Cuchullain's men turned from thoughts of battle to the preparation of a feast. The deer were brought, the pit lined with peat and set alight. The deer were prepared and then laid on the polished stones.

Cuchullain leaned on his spear and spoke to Carril, the grey-haired bard. "Is this feast prepared for me alone? The King of Lochlin is on our shore, far from the deer of Lochlin's hills. Go you, Carril, to Swaran and invite him to our feast."

So Carril, famed user of words, descended to the shore and spoke to Swaran of Cuchullain's invitation.

Swaran did not hesitate in his reply. "Though all the daughters of Erin should extend to me their snow-white arms, their breasts heaving, and their eyes expressing love, still, as solid as the rocks of Lochlin shall Swaran remain. And, in the morning, the eastern sun shall light me the way to Cuchullain's death. Let dark Cuchullain yield to me King Cormac's ancient throne, or Erin's torrents will run with the red foam of your chieftain's pride."

Disappointed, Carril returned to his lord.

"No feast, Carril, is complete without your tales of former times," said Cuchullain to him. "Drive away the night with your songs."

So Carril took up his harp and sang of the heroes of old.

The ghosts of the lately dead were near. And throughout the land of Erin, the feeble voices of those dead were heard.

Woden's Day

As the sun slowly began its rise in the east, Connal saw two ravens circling the bodies of the dead on the battlefield.

Connal took himself away from the other warriors and lay beneath an ancient tree beside a mountain stream. Its peaceful murmur was soothing after the previous day's sounds of battle. A stone covered in moss was his pillow.

To him appeared the shade of Crugal. It was Swaran himself who had robbed Crugal of his life. Now Crugal's face was white as the moon, his robes like clouds, his eyes two decaying flames. On his breast could be seen his wine dark wound.

"Crugal," said Connal, "why are you so pale and sad? It cannot be the pallor of fear, so what disturbs you?"

Crugar stood over the hero and stretched his pale hand out towards him. His voice was feeble, faint. "O, Connal, my ghost is in the cave of my native hills while my corpse is on the shore. Never shall we two talk in the land of the living. I see the dark cloud of death on our land. The sons of Erin shall fall."

The ghost faded away and Connal arose. He headed straight to his chieftain and wakened Cuchullain by striking his shield.

"I thought to kill the person who so wakened me," said Cuchullain. "I could have lost a good friend just now. Why do you wish to speak to me at this early hour?"

Said Connal, "The ghost of Crugal came to me from his dark dwelling. I could see the stars shine through his cloud-like form. His voice was quiet like the sound of a distant stream. He came as a messenger of death. Many of the men of Erin will rest forever in the dark and narrow house. Sue for peace, my chieftain, or let us retreat."

"Crugal spoke to you although stars twinkled through his form? O, Connal, it was merely the wind murmuring through the caves. Or, if indeed it was the form of Crugal, why did you not bring him to my sight? Did you enquire the location of his cave? I could take my sword and go there to force his knowledge from him. But that knowledge cannot be great, because today he was right here beside me. He could not have gone beyond these hills. So, who has told him of our deaths?"

"Ghosts fly on clouds and ride on wings," replied Connal. "They rest together in their caves and talk of mortal men."

"Then let them talk of mortal men, but not of Cuchullain, Erin's chief. Let them forget about me for I will not fly from Swaran. If I must fall, my tomb will be famous in future times. I do not fear death, but I fear to flee. Ask Fingal, for he has often seen my victories.

"Crugal, dim phantom of the hill, show yourself to me! I will not retreat!
"Go, Connal, and strike my shield with my spear. Let my heroes arise from their slumbers. If Fingal will not come to aid us, we shall still fight on and perhaps die in the battle of heroes."

When Connal left to summon the troops, Cuchullain glanced up and saw the two ravens and pondered the meaning of that sight.

Responding to the sound of the shield, the heroes arose like a forest of stout oak. The clouds were grey that morning and the blue grey mist swam slowly around the mountains, hiding the sons of Erin.

Likewise, Swaran woke his troops and addressed them. "Let us pursue the sons of Erin over the plains. Morla, I will have you go to young King Cormac's halls and bid him yield to Swaran before his people fall into their tombs and all his hills are silent."

The dark shades of Autumn flew over the grassy hills. Gloomy and dark also came Lochlin's warriors. And, leading them, taller than any one of them, was their King with his shield reflecting the light of the risen sun.

Suddenly the mist cleared and all Cuchullain's men appeared like an impassable ridge of rocks.

Swaran spoke once more to Morla. "Offer these men the same terms we give to kings when nations bow before us whose valiant fighters are all dead and virgins fill the fields with their weeping."

Morla rode towards his enemies and repeated his King's words to Cuchullain. "Give to Swaran Erin's lovely plains and give over to him your spouse and famous dog. Your wife who is both stately and beautiful, your dog who can outpace the wind. Give these to us as proof of your weakness and we will let you live."

It is said that a smile crossed Cuchullain's lips. "Tell proud Swaran that Cuchullain never yields. Swaran can have the dark blue ocean to sail away on, or the green fields of Erin to bury his dead. No stranger will ever have my lovely wife's embrace until the deer run faster than nimble footed Luath."

"Vain charioteer," said Morla, "would you fight a King whose many ships could carry off the spoils of your entire island? That is how little Erin means to the King of the Ocean."

"King Cormac shall rule this emerald isle while Connal and Cuchullain live. Connal, you've heard what Morla has to say. Do you still argue for peace? O, spirit of Crugal, why did you fill our minds with thoughts of death? Come, my warriors, raise your spears and bows and let us engage with this proud foe."

At that, Carril the bard began to sing of ancient victories and thus the spirits of ancient warriors filled the minds of Cuchullain's heroes.

Then dismal, roaring, fierce, and deep the gloom of battle began. Mighty Cuchullain took the lead on his chariot and his heroes followed him like a torrent pouring off the hills.

Just then, Degrena, the spouse of fallen Crugal, rushed into the ranks of his murderers. Thus she joined her husband in the hall of sorrows. Her father, Cairbar, saw her fall and his roar rose above the sounds of battle. In his fury he began to down the forces of Lochlin from wing to wing.

Cuchullain, too, cut down the foe like a scythe through a field of thistles. But Swaran himself cut down many of Erin's great warriors. Cairbar joined his daughter, while Curach, Morglan, and Ca-olt also died.

To right and left Cuchullain saw his friends dying like snow melting in the sun. Grumal witnessed his comrades striving pointlessly like reeds against the wind. He fled like a stag from the hunter, but few were they who joined this leader of soulless men.

Cuchullain spoke to Connal. "O, first of mortal men, you foretold me of this slaughter. But, though Grumal leads his followers away, shall we not fight on?" Then he turned to Carril and said, "Carril, lead the living to that bushy hill while Connal and I shall stand together and save our retreating friends."

Connal leapt onto Cuchullain's chariot and together they defended the rear. Like waves behind the whale behind them rushed the foe.

Finally, on the wooded hill, Erin's sons were granted a pause. Cuchullain dismounted and leaned against a mighty oak.

Moran, son of Fithil, had meanwhile kept his eye upon the sea. Now he rode like lightning to tell Cuchullain his news.

"The ships," he cried, "the ships of the Lonely Isle. Fingal comes, the breaker of shields. The waves foam before his black prows, his sails like swift moving clouds."

"Blow, you winds," said Cuchullain, "that rush o'er this misty isle. Your sails, O Fingal, are to me like the clouds of morning, your ships like the light of the sun, and you like a pillar of fire. Let us spend the night here, Connal, and await the arrival of Fingal."

Winds whistled through the woods where the warriors of Erin rested. Rain clouds gathered above. And sad, by the side of a rushing stream, sat Cuchullain of the hundred battles.

Thor's Day

Lightning announced an early start to the day. Deafening thunder shook the very ground. Rain bathed the dead on the plain and their once foaming blood turned to rivers.

The rain gradually ceased and Carril the bard lifted his harp. Fingal was coming, he who had fought Lochlin in the past and had won. Carril sang the tale of this conflict.

At that time, the King of Lochlin was Starno, father of Swaran. Fingal had before captured this King in battle. Instead of killing him, Fingal had released him to sail back to Lochlin, one King showing mercy to another.

Some years later, Starno was sitting in his great hall with his bard, Snivan of the grey locks. "Snivan, go thou to Morven and offer Fingal my daughter's hand in marriage. She is the fairest of the fair and her soul is generous and mild. Tell all this to Fingal and invite him and his bravest heroes to our halls."

Snivan did as the King requested and Fingal assembled his men and headed on their ships to Lochlin.

"Welcome," said Starno, "welcome, King of Rocky Morven. Wecome, you heroes, sons of the Lonely Isle. Three days within my halls shall you feast. Three days shall we hunt the boars of my kingdom. This way your fame will reach the ears of my daughter, the fair maid Agandecca."

But, in reality, Starno had plotted to kill them. Fingal had already had doubts about Starno's generosity and had kept on his battle dress.

But soon the shells were filled with wine and all began to enjoy the feast. The trembling harps told tales of joy. Bards sang of heroes in battle and of men in love.

Fingal's bard Ullin was with the company. He sang in praise of Agandecca and the King of Morven. Agandecca heard all this and left her apartments to join the heroes in her father's hall.

Fingal saw this vision of the daughter of the snow kingdom. Her complexion was as fair as the shining moon, her steps like the music of songs. And when she saw Fingal, she fell in love at once. Her soul let out a sigh. She lowered her modest eyes.

On the third day, the sun shone brightly in the woods. They spent half the day in the chase. Starno of the dark brows saw Fingal capture many boars, his spear red with their blood.

Back at the castle, Agandecca came to Fingal's chambers, her blue eyes filled with tears.

"Fingal, trust not my father's prideful heart. Within that wood he has hidden his warriors. Beware the wood of death. But remember me, Agandecca, and save me from the wrath of my father."

Seeming unconcerned, Fingal returned with his men to the woods. Starno's warriors were found and swiftly killed. Fingal returned to confront Starno.

Back in his halls, Starno's dark brows were like storm clouds, his eyes like meteors at night. "Bring my daughter to the King of Morven whose hand is stained with the blood of my people. Her words to him have not been in vain."

Agandecca arrived, her eyes red with tears, her raven locks hanging loose. Her breast heaved with sighs. She approached her father who pierced her side with his sword. At once she fell dead.

Fingal and his men took out their swords. The hall resounded to the sounds of battle and Starno either fled or died, depending who is telling the tale.

Fingal took Agandecca back to his ship. Her tomb is still in Morven, the sea roars around her dark dwelling.

After this recital, Cuchullain remarked, "Lochlin shall fall again this day before the King of Morven. O, moon, show your face among the clouds and light his white sails."

Calmar, the son of Matha, had been badly wounded but still made it up the hill. He spoke to Connal and Cuchullain. "Calmar is bold as my fathers. Danger flies from his uplifted sword. They best succeed who dare. But, Cuchullain, should I become a lifeless corpse, remember me. Place me beside some stone of remembrance that future times may hear my fame."

"Son of Matha," said Cuchullain, "I will never abandon thee. I rejoice in an unequal field of battle, my soul increases in danger. Go, Calmar, greet Fingal and bid him hasten like the sun after a storm."

Calmar left on his mission and Cuchullain moved to a place where he could be by himself. His face was pale and he leaned on his father's spear. He remembered his mother's sadness at her husband's fall.

Now from the grey mists of the ocean, the white-sailed ships of Fingal appeared. Swaran saw them from his encampment on the hill. Swaran ordered his forces to turn away from the depleted sons of Erin to face the warriors of Fingal.

Meanwhile, bending, weeping, sad, and slow, and dragging his long spear behind him, Cuchullain sank down and mourned his fallen friends. He became ashamed to face Fingal who regarded him as a warrior of renown.

"How many lie there of my friends? They that were so cheerful in the hall not long ago. No more will I hear their steps in the heath, or hear their voices in the chase of the deer.

Pale, silent, low on bloody beds are they now. O, spirits of the lately dead, follow Cuchullain to his cave in Tura. There, remote from the battle, I shall lie unknown. No bard shall hear of me, no grey stone shall be raised to my renown. Mourn me with the lowly dead. Departed is my fame."

Fingal had arrived on the beach holding his bright lance. "Behold the blood of my friends on the field. Is Cuchullain no more? Ryno and Fillan, my sons, ascend that hill beyond the shore and sound Fingal's war horn. Let Swaran know I await him. Let him bring his entire race, for strong in battle are the friends of the dead."

Fingal's sons flew like lightning to their task. All heard the horn announcing Fingal's war. Swaran led his men to battle. Wrath burned in his face, his eyes announced his valour.

Fingal saw him in the vanguard and thought at once of Swaran's sister Agandecca. When she was killed by her own father, Swaran's youthful tears mourned his lost sister.

Fingal summoned his bard, Ullin, and instructed him to meet with Swaran and ask him to join Fingal in a feast. He had no hatred for Swaran, the brother of the first woman he had ever loved.

Ullin conveyed this message to the King of Lochlin. "Come to my King's feast and pass the day in rest. Time enough for battle another day."

"Today!" said Starno's wrathful son, "we shall break your echoing shields. Tomorrow my feast will be spread while Fingal lies in the earth."

When Fingal heard this response, he addressed his warriors. "Tomorrow let him have his feast if he can, for today we send his men to their deaths. Ossian, my son, stand at my side. Gaul, lift thy terrible sword. Fergus, bend your bow. Fillan, prepare to throw your lance through the sky like a meteor. All of you, lift your shields to hide the sun. Follow me and equal my deeds in battle."

Soon the groans of the battle spread over the hills and a thousand ghosts shrieked at once on the hollow wind.

Fingal led his men. He was a hard act to follow. Ryno's sword was a pillar of fire. Dark was the brow of Gaul whom none could stop. Fergus rushed forward like the unstoppable gale. Fillan moved unseen by his foes as if he were the air itself. And many a foe fell before Ossian.

The autumn night came swiftly and the battle paused. Fingal dined and listened to his bard. His grandson, Ossian's child, Oscar, was by his side.

You fought well today, Oscar," said his grandfather. "You remind me of when I was young in battle. Take heed of this: never search for a battle, nor shun it when it comes."

Gaul then approached his King. Once it had been thought that he, Gaul, would be King of Morven. But in time the clan accepted Fingal and Gaul, once a rival, became his close friend as well as a great hero.

"Fingal," said Gaul, "let me make a request. Sheathe your sword and let your people fight. We are as nothing if the bards don't sing of our brave deeds. Just now, they will sing only of you. When the morning breaks, watch our brave deeds at a distance. Let Swaran feel the strength of my sword."

"Nothing would please me more," replied Fingal, "than to hear songs of your fame. Lead you shall, but my spear shall be near to aid you if you are in the midst of danger." Fingal then turned to the bard and the other musicians. "With your songs," he said, "lull me into sleep. Maybe my love Agandecca is near her kin from Lochlin and maybe she will come to my dreams."

Freya's Day

Everallin, not long dead, wife of Ossian and mother of Oscar, appeared to her husband as he roused himself.

"O, Ossian," she cried, "rise up and save our son. He fights alone with Lochlin's warriors. Save him." And with that she faded back into the morning mist.

Ossian put on his battle gear. Oscar had been sent during the night to keep an eye on the enemy, but eventually they had spotted him and he was now in great danger. Ossian began to loudly sing tales of the heroes of old and his voice seemed to the battling warriors as the sound of distant thunder. Seeing his foes momentarily distracted, Oscar fled.

Fingal started from his dream of Agandecca. He stood up and leaned on Trenmor's shield, the shield which had seen so many battles.

While recovering from his vision of his first love, Fingal heard steps approach. It was Ossian and Oscar. Fingal noticed that Ossian was already dressed in his battle gear.

"What have you come to report, Ossian? Are our foes ready to surrender? Are their tall ships sailing back to Lochlin? Or are they preparing again for battle?"

Just as Oscar was about to speak, Fingal raised his hand. "Ah! I hear their voices on the morning wind. Oscar, run across the heath, awake our warriors, and get them to prepare for battle."

Fingal readied himself to address his troops. At the sound of his voice, the deer were startled in the woods, the rocks shook with the noise. The heroes were glad to hear the voice of

Fingal, for often had he led them in the fight and they had returned with precious spoils.

"Prepare, my heroes, for the death of thousands this day. Gaul shall lead thee, so that his fame will be told in future songs. I shall be on yonder hill. My sword is ever ready, but my wish is that you never need it.

"I call on you, the ghosts of our mighty dead, ye riders of the storm. Receive with joy my fallen people and bring them to your hills. May they come to my silent dreams and delight my soul in its rest.

"Fillan and Oscar, advance with valour to the fight. Behold you all, the son of Morni, Brave Gaul! Let your swords be like his in the strife and behold the deeds of his hands. Protect the friends of your fathers and remember the chiefs of old."

Fingal then headed to the top of the hill and three bards accompanied him to carry his words to the heroes. Then, with a wave of his sword, the warriors descended to the battlefield.

Oscar's face beamed with joy as he spoke to his father. "Mighty father, go you with Fingal and give me a chance of fame. And, if I should fall, remember that lonely sunbeam of my love, the white-haired daughter of Toscar."

"Oscar, I would rather you built your father a tomb. I will not yield the fight to thee. For, first and bloodiest in the war, my arm shall teach thee how to fight. And should I fall, remember, my son, to place this sword, this bow, and this horn within that dark and narrow house whose mark is one grey stone. I have no love to leave behind since my beloved Everallin, thy mother, is no more."

Then both turned to hear the voice of Gaul who waved on high his father's sword and rushed to his fate.

Man met with man. Shields broke and men fell. As a hundred hammers on the son of the furnace, so rang a thousand swords.

As stones that break on the rocks, as trees fall to the blows of the axe, as thunder rolls from hill to hill, so the battle raged.

Swaran's army seemed to retreat, but then Fingal beheld Swaran himself engage with Gaul. Fingal half-rose from his position on the hill at that sight and half-assumed his spear. He addressed Ullin, the bard.

"Go, Ullin, my aged bard. Sing to Gaul the songs of his fathers' wars. Song enlivens war and when he hears your stories, Gaul will not yield."

When Gaul heard the song of Ullin, his spirits were uplifted. But then Swaran cleft Gaul's shield in twain and Fingal's warriors had to retreat before the might of Swaran.

But then they heard the mighty voice of Fingal himself. They stood still, their red faces bent to the earth, ashamed at their actions. Swaran too stopped to listen.

"Raise your standards," boomed the voice of Fingal. "As they flutter in the wind, let them remind us of our great task."

The standards were raised and each hero's spirits lifted.

"Let every chief among you now choose one of Lochlin's bands."

At that, Gaul and Oscar and all the chieftains shouted the names of the foes they chose to conquer.

Then Fingal shouted to the King of Lochlin. "Those warriors' names are the choices of my heroes. But, Swaran, you yourself are the choice of Fingal."

Thus did the tide of battle turn.

It then so happened that Fingal killed one of the heroes of Lochlin. As the grey-haired warrior rolled in the dust, he lifted his faint eyes to Fingal and Fingal recognised him.

"Is it by me thou hast fallen?" lamented Fingal. "In the bloody halls of Starno I once beheld your tears for Agandecca. You were the foe of my foe and now you have fallen by my hand. Ullin, this is Mathon. Raise a grave for him and add his name to the song of Agandecca."

From his cave, Cuchullain heard these sounds of battle. He called on Connal and Carril to observe the fight for him. Cuthullain's desire for fighting was kindled and darkness gathered on his brow. His hand was on the sword of his fathers and his eyes yearned to see his foes. Three times he attempted to rush to battle, and three times Connal stopped him.

"Great chieftain of the Isle of Mist," he said, "Fingal subdues the foe. Do not you seek the part of the fame of the King."

Reminded thus of his duty, Cuthullain addressed Carril. "Go thou and greet the King of Morven, when the army of Lochlin falls away like a stream after rain and the noise of battle is over. Praise Fingal, king of swords. Give him this sword of mine, for no longer is Cuthullain worthy to lift up his fathers' arms.

"O, ye souls of chiefs of ancient days, be you the companions of Cuchullain! Talk to him in his cave of sorrow. For never more shall I be renowned among the mighty in the land. I am like a beam which once shone, a mist that has faded away."

Connal saw how despondent Cuchullain was and spoke to him. "Why that gloom, my chief? Our friends are mighty in the battle. Already renowned are you among warriors. Many were the foes who met their deserved deaths at your hand. Many are the songs the bards sing of your exploits.

"Behold the King of Morven. He moves through the enemy like a pillar of fire.

"O, Fingal, happy are your people. You fight our battles. You step up to every danger. In the days of peace we listen to your wise words. You speak and thousands obey. Those who dare to challenge us tremble at the sound of your steel.

"But look now, Cuchullain. Who is that who dares to challenge Fingal himself? It is none other than Swaran, son of Starno. Behold the battle of the chiefs!"

Every blow in this battle was like the hundred hammers of the furnace! Terrible was the Battle of the Kings! Their dark-brown shields were cleft in twain, their swords both broken from the blows on the warriors' helms. They both flung away their weapons and grasped each other. They embraced in a clench and each tried to throw the other to the ground.

Even the strongest branch reaches breaking point. And at last Swaran fell.

Fingal called to his supporters. "There lies Swaran in defeat. Bind him and guard him with care, for still he has the strength of a thousand boars. He has been raised to fight and his race for generations is a race of warriors.

"Gaul, you remain in charge of the King of Lochlin. Oscar, Fillan, Ryno, pursue the rest of his army."

They flew then like lightning over the heath.

A chief of Lochlin then slowly approached Fingal.

"Tell me, youth," asked Fingal, "art thou of Fingal's foes?"

"I am indeed a son of Lochlin," said he. "Strong was my arm in war. My spouse is weeping at home, but her Orla will never return."

"Do you fight on or yield? No foe will overcome me, but my friends are welcome in my banqueting hall. Son of the Waves, follow me. Dine with us and then we will go and hunt the deer."

"I will not yield. My sword has always been unmatched, so let the King of Morven yield."

"Orla, I never yielded to any man. Draw your sword and choose your opponent. For many are my heroes."

"And does the King himself refuse the combat? Fingal, alone of his race, is a match for Orla.

"But if I should fall before Fingal, as every warrior must at some time die, send over the waves my sword to my wife, so that she may show it to our son to kindle his soul to war."

"That is a mournful tale, Orla. One day, indeed, all warriors must die and their children inherit their useless weapons. But Orla, I shall raise your tomb and send your spouse your sword if so it turns out."

And so they fought. Feeble was the arm of Orla. The sword of Fingal descended and cleft his shield in two. It fell from Orla's side and glittered on the ground like broken glass.

"King of Morven," said the hero, "lift thy sword and pierce my heart. Wounded and faint from the battle, my friends have left me here. My mournful tale will be told to my wife, alone in the wood by the banks of the stream, her tears dropping on the grass."

"No," said Fingal, "I will never wound thee, Orla. Let your spouse meet you by that stream when you return from war. Let thy grey-haired father – perhaps he is blind with age? – hear the voice of his son in the hall."

"Never will that happen, Fingal. On this heath must I die. Only foreign bards may sing of me. My broad belt has been hiding my wound. Now I will throw this belt to the wind."

The dark blood poured from his side and he fell pale on the heath. Fingal bent over him as he died, then called for his young heroes.

"Oscar and Fillan, in your songs remember brave Orla. Here let this hero rest, far from his spouse. Let us lay him here in the narrow house. His sons shall find his bow at home, but will not be able to bend it. His faithful dogs will howl on the hills. The boars which he used to hunt will rejoice."

Fingal then looked again at Oscar and Fillan. "Where is Ryno, your young brother? Why is he the last to come to his father?"

"Ryno," said Ullin, "is with the shades of his fathers. He, also, lies on this heath."

"The swiftest in the race," sighed Fingal, "has he fallen? O, Ryno, you were too young. I was still getting to know you. Sleep softly, Ryno. Fingal shall soon see you again. The bards will tell of Fingal's fame, but Ryno, you did not live long enough to receive your fame. Ullin, strike your harp for Ryno. Sing ye what would have been. Farewell, thou first in every field. No more shall I send you off to battle. You were so fair and now I see you not. Farewell."

Then Fingal pointed to some nearby tombs.

"Four stones covered with moss are there to mark the narrow houses of death. Near them let my Ryno rest, so that he will be neighbour to the valiant. Fillan and Fergus, bring hither Orla. Not unequal shall Ryno be when Orla is by his side."

Fingal and his followers then returned to where Gaul and Ossian were holding Swaran. Fingal's brow was gloomy and everyone felt his pain. He had, indeed, been victorious in the fight, but his joy was mixed with grief.

Seeing Fingal like that, Carril approached Ossian instead. "Cuchullain's thoughts are on the battle he has lost. He is mourning the departure of his fame that fled like the mist."

"Hail, Carril," said Ossian. "Your voice is like the harp in the halls of Tura. Thy words are pleasant as the shower that replenishes the fruits of the field. Please, sit now on the heath, O Bard, and let us hear thy voice sing the tales of happier days."

The clouds of night rolled down over the hills and the stars in the north peeked through. A distant wind could be heard in the woods, but silent and dark was the plain of death.

Carril sang of the heroes of the past and their ghosts returned in joy at the sound of the harp.

A huge feast had been prepared. A thousand oaks had been felled for the fires. The warriors' vessels were filled with the best of drinks and their hearts began to fill again with joy. But Fingal was silent.

Fingal leaned on his ancient shield, his grey locks stirring in the wind. He gazed at Swaran and saw the grief of that foreign King.

When Carril finished, Fingal called to Ullin. "Raise the Song of Peace, Ullin, and soothe my battle-weary soul, that my ears may forget the noise of arms. Let the harmony of a hundred harps gladden us. That sound never left Fingal saddened. Trenmor, thy flashing sword is strong in battle, but peaceful it rests by my side when the war is over."

Ullin sang of Trenmor, great grandfather to Fingal, and his marriage to Inibaca, daughter of yet another King of Lochlin. Hearing this, Fingal turned to address Lochlin's present King.

"Swaran, our families have just met in battle, but often in the past have we feasted in each other's halls. Now let thy face brighten with gladness and thine ear delight in the harp. Tomorrow raise your white sails to the wind, thou brother of Agandecca. You once wept for her in Starno's halls. Now, for her sake, you may depart on the morrow like the sun setting in the west. Or would you rather face me in combat a final time?"

"King of Morven," replied the King, "Never again will Swaran fight with thee. I have indeed seen thee in my father's halls, and few were your years beyond mine. When shall I, I said to myself back then, lift the spear like the noble Fingal?

"But many of Lochlin's ships have lost their youths in this land. Take my hands, O King of Morven, and be the friend of Swaran. When your sons in the future come to my land, there shall be feasting in the halls and the sport of the chase in the valleys."

"I shall not," said mighty Fingal, "take even one of your ships. Nor do I ever want to conquer your land. This land here, its woods, its deer, is enough for me. You were a faithful brother to Agandecca. Sail away in the morning and return to your native land."

"Blessed be thy soul, O King," said Swaran. "In war you are the mountain storm, but in peace the breeze of Spring. Take my hands in friendship.

"Let thy bards mourn those who fell. Let Erin place the sons of Lochlin in the earth that hereafter the children of the north may behold the place where their fathers fought. Thus our fame shall last forever."

And again a hundred harps accompanied the tales of other days.

At length, Fingal addressed Carril. "Where is Cuchullain? I have not seen him at our feast."

"Cuchullain," said Carril to his King, "lies in his dreary cave, his thoughts on the battles he has lost. He sends this sword to you, for you have scattered all his foes. Take, O Fingal, his sword, for the fame of Cuchullain has departed like mist before the wind in the valley."

"No," replied the King. "Fingal shall never take his sword. His arm is mighty in war, so his fame shall never fail. Many have been overcome in battle that have shone afterwards like the son of heaven. Go tell him this."

Saturn's Day

In the morning, Swaran summoned his warriors with the sound of his horn. Silent and sad they boarded their ships. White, like the crest of a thousand waves, their sails departed the land of Erin.

Then Fingal announced the deer hunt. "Call the dogs to me, lovers of the chase. Call white-breasted Bran and the swift-moving Luath, Cuchullain's dog. Call Fillan and Ryno... but he is no longer here. My son is on his bed of death. Fillan and Fergus, blow my horn that the joy of the chase may begin. Let those deer know that we are coming!"

The shrill sound spread through the woods. A thousand dogs joined their masters and flew through the woods at once. A deer fell by every dog and three by white-breasted Bran. He brought these to his master Fingal that his master's joy in the hunt may be great.

One deer fell near the tomb of Ryno and the grief of Fingal returned. He saw how peaceful lay the headstone of him who had always been first at the hunt.

"No more shall you rise, my son, to take part in our feasts. Soon will thy tomb be hidden and the grass grow rank on your grave. The sons of the weak shall pass over it and shall not know that the mighty lie there."

When the hunt was over, Fingal summoned Ossian, Oscar, Fillan, and Gaul. "Let us ascend the hill to the cave of Tura and find Cuchullain. Come, let us find the king of swords and restore him to joy."

On hearing this, Connan of the small renown thought to join them.

They climbed the hill against the wind and finally found the cave and the great warrior. Cuchullain was leaning heavily on his sword when he spotted Fingal.

"Hail, O breaker of the shields!"

"Hail to thee, Fingal," replied Cuchullain. "Hail to all the sons of Morven. Delightful to me is thy presence, O Fingal. It is like the welcoming sunbeams on the hill. Your sons are like the stars which give you light in the night-time. It is not often that you find me like this."

"Many are your words," said Connan, "but where are your warlike deeds? Why did we come over the sea to aid thy feeble sword? You flew to your cave of sorrow while Connan had to fight your battles. Give me your weapons that I may use them in the next battles."

"I fled not to the cave of sorrows," replied Cuchullain, "as long as Erin's warriors lived."

"Connan," said Fingal, "say no more. Cuchullain has been long renowned in battle and often have the songs been sung of his fame.

"Now, Cuchullain, shall you soon sail back into the arms of your wife Bragela. Her tender eye is now in tears. She listens every night to hear the songs of your rowers, to hear the song of the sea and the voices of the harps."

"Long shall she listen in vain, O Fingal. Cuchullain shall never return. How can I let Bragela see me like this? Fingal, always before I was victorious in battle, but now..."

"And hereafter thou shalt be victorious again. The fame of Cuchullain will grow like the branches on a mighty tree. Many battles await thee, many songs to be sung in your name.

"Oscar, let us prepare for more feasting that our souls may rejoice and the dangers we faced be forgotten."

They took Cuchullain down the hill and he joined them in their feasting. The strength of his arm returned, his dark thoughts faded, and gladness brightened his face.

Thus the night was passed in feasting and song.

Sun's Day

In the morning, Fingal raised his spear for all to see and thus he led his warriors to the shore.

"Let us spread our sails to catch the wind and sail for Morven."

So they rowed and sang and sped with joy through the foam of the ocean.

Characters, Places, Animals, Gods

Characters in order of appearance

CUCHULLAIN
CORMAC – King of Ulster, still in his minority at the time of this story
CARBAR – previous foe of Cuchullain
MORAN – one of Cuchullain's messengers
FITHIL – father of Moran
SWARAN/GARBH/GARVE – King of Lochlin aka Jutland
FINGAL
CABAIT – grandfather of Cuchullain
CONNAL – warrior on Cuchullain's side
CRUGAL – warrior on Cuchullain's side
FAVI – father of Ronnar
RONNAR – warrior on Cuchullain's side
CALMAR – warrior on Cuchullain's side
MATHA – father of Calmar
CATHBAT – previously fallen warrior
DUCHOMAR – previously fallen warrior
MORNA – lover of both warriors above
ARNO'S SON – a messenger of Swaran
CRUGAL – one of Cuchullain's warriors killed by Swaran
TRENAR
CARRIL – one of Cuchullain's bards
MORLA – a messenger of Swaran
DEGRENA – wife of Crugal
CAIRBAR – Degrena's father
CURACH
MORGLAN
CA-OLT
GRUMAL – a cowardly warrior who fled from Swaran
STARNO – previous King of Lochlin, father of Swaran and Agandecca
SNIVAN – Starno's bard

AGANDECCA – daughter of Starno, in love with Fingal
ULLIN – Fingal's bard
RYNO – son of Fingal
FILLAN – son of Fingal
OSSIAN – son of Fingal, warrior, bard, father of Oscar, latterly referred to as "an deigh na feinne", the last of his race, held to be the reciter/composer of these tales
GAUL – once a challenger for the kingship of Morven, but now one of Fingal's most faithful friends
FERGUS – Fingal's bowman
OSCAR – Ossian's son
EVERALLIN – late wife of Ossian
TRENMOR – great grandfather of Fingal
MORNI – father of Gaul
TOSCAR – beloved of Oscar
MATHON – one of Swaran's warriors, killed by Fingal
ORLA – one of Swaran's warriors, killed by Fingal
INIBACA – wife of Trenmor, daughter of a previous king of Lochlin
CONNAN – one of Fingal's warriors
BRAGELA – wife of Cuchullain
LUGAR – one of Cuchullain's warriors

Places

TURA/TARA – ancient capital of Erin, said to be located between the rivers Boyne and Liffey
ULSTER – part of the kingdom of Dalriada, in Erin
LOCHLIN – Jutland/Denmark = Land of Lakes
ERIN – ancient name for Ireland (= Erin's Land), after the goddess Ériu
INNISFAIL – another name for Ireland (innis = island)
INNISTORE – Island of Whales = Orkney, ruled from Skandinavia until 1472
ISLE OF MIST - Skye
MORVEN – ancient territory of Argyle, northern part of Dalriada

Animals

BRAN – Fingal's dog
LUATH – Cuchullain's dog, after whom Robert Burns named his dog and one of the dogs in his poem The Twa Dogs
DUSRONNAL – one of the steeds who pulled Cuchullain's chariot
SIFADDA – another of the steeds who pulled Cuchullain's chariot

Gods

No gods are mentioned explicitly in these sagas, but occasionally there are allusions to the Norse Gods. We still use these gods as the basis for our days of the week, so they have been used here to indicate the passage of time in this war.

TYR/TIW – god of war
WODEN/ODIN – leader of the Norse gods, often accompanied by two ravens
THOR – god of thunder, son of Odin and Freya
FREYA/FRIGG – wife of Odin
SATURN – aka Cronos, creator of all gods

Macpherson's Tales of Ossian

Fingal is only one of a number of the Tales of Ossian. The stories which Macpherson included in his various editions are:

Cath-Loda – Fingal, when young, encounters Starno and Swaran

Comala – This dramatic poem mentions Caracul; if this is Caracalla, it dates the events to 211CE. Comala is the daughter of Starno, king of Inistore (Orkney). She disguises herself as a youth to follow Fingal.

Carric-Thura – This is the palace of Cathulla, another king of Inistore. Here Ossian mentions "the circle of Loda". This seems to have been a place of worship for the Scandinavians, Loda being their god Odin.

Carthon – Carthon is the son of Moina and Clessámor. Carthon is unwittingly killed by his father.

Oina-Morul – This is the name of a girl who is offered to Ossian as the result of a battle. But he restores her to her beloved.

Colna-Dona – Colna-Dona meets Toscar at the raising of a stone to a battle. They fall in love.

Oithona – Oithona is the daughter of Nuäth. She falls in love with Gaul, is kidnapped, and tragically killed during a rescue mission. William Blake, a huge admirer of Macpherson, seems to have taken some character names from this story for his own Visions of the Daughters of Albion.

Croma – Croma is part of Ireland. Malvina, daughter of Toscar is grieving over the death of her lover Oscar. Ossian diverts her with a story.

Calthon and Colmal – These are the two sons of Rathmor. They are adopted by Dunthalmo who had killed their father. They seek revenge.

The War of Caros – Caros is attacked by Oscar while repairing the wall of Agricola.

Cathlin of Clutha – The Clutha is the river Clyde. This is the story of the kidnapping of Cathlin.

Sub-Malla of Lumon – A continuation of the above.

The War of Inis-Thona – Inis-Thona is a Scandinavian island. It concerns a young Ossian.

The Songs of Selma – Selma is the royal residence. The poem is an address to the evening star.

Fingal – The story of Fingal and Cuthullin and their battle with Swaran.

Lathmon – A British prince tries to invade Morven. But when Fingal returns from Ireland...

Dar-Thula – Cuthullin has died. There ensues another unfortunate love story.

The Death of Cuthullin – Cuthullin is slain in battle.

The Battle of Lora – In 1813, this poem was published in Russian in St Petersburg, which shows the continuing interest in Macpherson outside of Scotland. Fingal has neglected to invite two fellow chieftains to a feast. They take their revenge.

Temora – Cairbar has murdered Cormac, king of Ireland. Fingal resolves to restore the rightful royal family to the throne.

Conlath and Cuthona – Conlath is in love with Cuthona. She is abducted by Toscar. Conlath is killed in the consequent battle and Cuthona dies of grief.

Berrathon – This is a Scandinavian island where Ossian and Toscar win a battle. There are intimations of the death of Ossian.

The Doctor Johnson Controversy

Doctor Johnson claimed a number of things:

He asserted that Macpherson's whole enterprise was a hoax and could not possibly be based on Gaelic originals

He stated that there could be no Gaelic manuscripts more than 100 years old

He claimed that the English had civilised the Scots and introduced them to literature. He simply could not accept that culture could be indigenous to Scotland. And anyway, as a people, the Scots were prone to fabrication

Let us deal with, indeed refute, Johnson's arguments in order.

Macpherson's first response to Johnson was that 19 manuscripts in Gaelic had been displayed at Thomas Becket's bookshop in London in 1762, so that Johnson had simply not checked. Many years later, Derick Thomson located 12 (not 19) of these sources for Fingal and we shall return to his research later.

The Highland Society of London reported that the 19 MSS handed over to them in 1803 "were the same as those deposited by Macpherson in the shop of Becket, his publisher, in 1762. Among them was the Book of the Dean [of Lismore], whose preservation we thus owe in part to Macpherson". (Thomson, pg 74)

Johnson was also clearly unaware of collections of Gaelic works such as The Book of the Dean of Lismore (c. 1480-1551). In fact centuries before that many Celtic legends were written down by literate monks in Ireland. The Celts as a race seem to have been distrustful of script, preferring to rely on speech and properly trained memories, but Johnson was a man who had studied only written literature and knew nothing of the world's oral traditions.

As for indigenous Scottish culture... The editors of the Oxford Shakespeare have this to say about his Troilus and Cressida (c. 1602): "Shakespeare would also have known Robert Henryson's ... The Testament of Cresseid, in which Cressida, deserted by Diomedes, dwindles into a leprous beggar."

In ABC of Reading by Ezra Pound, the author is dismissive of the kind of prejudice shown by readers of literature from England (like Johnson): "The omission of [Gavin] Douglas from The Oxford Book of XVIth Century Verse sheds no credit on either the press or their anthologist ... Douglas wrote a quantity of original poetry, part of which is indubitably superior to a good deal they have included."

Henryson (c. 1420-c. 1490), Dunbar (c. 1460-c.1520), Douglas (c. 1474-1522), Blin Harry (c. 1450-1493) – and that is just some of the writers in Scots whom Johnson never refers to. But as well as them, Guillaume le Clerc (aka William Malveism, Bishop of St Andrews, d. 1238) wrote in French, as did Mary, Queen of Scots (1542-1587). And then there are the writers in Gaelic, a far more ancient language than English: Mugron, Abbot of Iona (d. 980), Muireadhach Albanach O Dalaigh (fl. 1200-1224), Aithbhreac Inghean Corcadail (fl. 1460s).

You no doubt feel I have made my point, and yet Johnson's errors are still quoted since people still think he always knew what he was talking about. But this is far from the only time when Johnson asserted something on a subject about which he knew nothing. He once stated that swallows "certainly sleep all winter ... in the bed of a river", repeating a nonsensical theory of the Swedish archbishop Olaus Magnus from 1555.

What, then, had James Macpherson done with the Gaelic tales? Are they, strictly, translations? How much of what we read is original and how much is actually Macpherson? It all hinges, again, on an understanding of the oral tradition and the role of an editor.

And, unfortunately, Macpherson was as guilty as Johnson in an unfair, illogical promotion of the prominence of his native land:

"Macpherson ... stressed that the Irish Ossianic ballads were borrowed from Scotland. As far as the Irish were concerned, however, the borrowing was the other way around. Whereas the reaction to Macpherson in England had been cries of forgery, in Ireland people were outraged that he tried to claim what they perceived as their poetry." (Blind Ossian's Fingal, p 40)

Macpherson's claim is, in fact, bunk.

There are two main cycles of Irish Sagas:
The Cù Chulainn / Ulster cycle (c. 1st century CE)
The Fenian / Finn / Ossianic cycle (c. 3rd century CE)

At first these were two separate collections of oral tales but then, in Viking times, the characters overlapped. This type of amalgamation of tales is common in the oral tradition from Homer to the Bible. As Will Storr points out in The Science of Storytelling: "the ragbag of ancient myths and fables become connected. The scribes turn them into one complete cause-and-effect laden tale."

Derick Thomson and the Gaelic Sources

Fingal

I said I would return to the research which Derick Thomson did. Here are the original sources of the work which became Fingal:

Book	Original Source
1	Garbh mac Stairn
2	Magnus (Manus)
3	Duan na h-Ingrinn (aka The Maid of Craca)
4,5,6	Fingal's visit to Norway Ossian's courtship
6	Sliabh nam Ban Fionn
Throughout	Praise of Goll Cù Chulainn's chariot

Book 4 is, in fact, very faithful to the original sources.

Macpherson's mistake was to claim that all these sources were part of an original Scottish "epic", equivalent to Homer and he makes this assertion very clear in his notes by frequent quotation from Homer and other classical sources. Ossian, old, blind, a bard, was, in fact, no less than Scotland's Homer!! Not quite.

I have two editions of Fingal, one at 66 pages and the other 89 pages. My editions of The Iliad have 436 pages (E. V. Rieu) and 583 pages (Robert Fitzgerald). Not that quantity is better than quality, but Fingal is certainly not "epic" in size. The Iliad is arranged in 24 "books" (we would use the word "chapters"), Fingal has 6. However, Homer (whoever he was) combined lots of old stories into one coherent whole which is what, in fact, Macpherson did. But to imply there was ever an original in Gaelic even as long as Fingal is simply false, or at least unprovable.

Macpherson's work is not a straightforward translation: "Macpherson's refining and bowdlerising pen has often changed the atmosphere of the ballads almost beyond recognition ... Macpherson's interest in defeat and melancholy may date back no further than the Rising of 1745 and the Battle of Culloden. His interest in wild nature, and his powerful if gloomy depictions of it, are not derived from an ancient Celtic source, but reflect the grey skies and rugged scenery of Badenoch." (Thomson, pg 84)

The Gaelic "Ossian" of 1807

Here Ossian's courting of Evirallin is close to the original ballads. In this episode, the Gaelic of 1807 could be genuinely ancient. But overall the 1807 edition is translated (with many flaws in the Gaelic) from Macpherson.

The Battle of Lora, or Teanntachd Mhór na Féinne

Here Macpherson "follows the sequence of his ballad source with some considerable fidelity". (Thomson, pg 42) But he edited out Saint Patrick.

The original Gaelic source:

La ga'n raibh Paidric na mhur
Gun salm air nidh ach agol
Chuaidh e thigh Ossan mhic Fhein
O's ann leis budh bhinn a ghloir.

One day when Saint Patrick was in his stronghold
Drinking, and in no mood for psalms
He went to the house of Oisein son of Finn
Since his talk was sweet (in his ears)

Macpherson thought that these ballads were corrupt because Saint Patrick could not, surely, have been drinking.

As usual, Macpherson blended the Teanntachd with other sources. After the main fight, Macpherson "makes Lorma, Aldo's former love, lament his death, and die eventually of grief. Aldo's ghost also appears. The ballads, unsentimental as always, quite forget about the deserted lady". (Thomson, pg 47)

Carthon

Here Macpherson "drew on the popular ballads on the death of Conloach. The ballad belongs to the Cù Chulainn rather than the Fionn cycle". (pg 48) "It is contrary to Macpherson's principles to tell a plain tale in a plain way." (pg 49) On the other hand, his 18th century audience could not be assumed to know the story of Cù Chullainn's past.

Dar-thula and the story of Deirdre

Deirdre is one of the oldest stories in the Scottish, not Irish, tradition. It dates back in MS to c. 13th century.

Macpherson has his own scheme of history and changes the names (and spellings) of people and places: Deirdre becomes Dar-thula; Naoise becomes Nathos; Ainnle becomes Althos.

In his preface, he alludes to Dar-thula in some sources committing suicide. This is indeed the case in the ballads.

"Macpherson may be said to adapt his sources with some ingenuity, but in so doing he loses much of the story. The representation becomes blurred. The fine clear colours of the original are gone – we no longer see the red blood and the black raven against the whiteness of the snow. At times, indeed, the course of the story becomes hard to follow. In this telling the tale has lost its tragedy, its pathos, its dignity, and practically all its meaning." (Thomson, pg 55)

Calthon and Colmal

No resemblance here to any known ballads.

Temora

Only in Book 1 is there any original Gaelic source. The rest has been made up by Macpherson and suffers badly from his style of writing.

The Battle of Gabhra was, in the original, the final downfall of Finn and the Fians.

Macpherson does not seem to understand that the 500 are not followers of Oscar – they are his opponents! This, by itself, of course, proves that he was looking at an original Gaelic source which he had misinterpreted. Says Thomson, "This may give us a clue to much of the confusion and vagueness of Macpherson's borrowings from Gaelic – he was not sufficiently conversant with the written language to grasp the exact details of the story." (pg 63)

Macpherson's assertion that Fingal etc. were of Scottish, not Irish, origin flies in the face of all the evidence. He outlines his historical system in his 1762 edition, but we can compare this to Foras Feasa ar Éirinn [History of Ireland], by Geoffrey Keating, Irish Texts Society, c. 1634, Vols IV, VIII, IX, and XV. Thomson says that a "comparison of his [Macpherson's] history with theirs shows the same curious blend of misreading and wilful misrepresentation which has already been noticed in his handling of some of the ballads". (pg 70)

"Macpherson had discovered from O'Flaherty [Roderick O'Flaherty, one of the first Irish historians from1685] and Keating that Fingal and his heroes were real characters in the history of Ireland, whose time era was from the middle to the end of the third century. In appropriating those heroes to the Highlands of Scotland, he found a convenient chasm in the history of Britain under the Romans, and connected Fingal with Caracalla in 208, and with Carausius the usurper in 286, to ascertain his era without recourse to Ireland, and escape detection during the intermediate period." (Thomson, pg 71) Cf. The History of Scotland, by Malcolm Laing, London, 1800, Vol. II pg 379.

What Macpherson did do in his best-selling books was introduce the world of Gaelic oral stories to a world which until that time was largely unaware of them. The close study of Gaelic languages and literature really takes off from this point and owes that to Macpherson. And, of course, his works are the real origins of Romanticism.

Macpherson's Method of Composition

Although Macpherson's work is indeed based on original Gaelic sources, he did not simply translate the material which he found. (Nor is Ezra Pound's Cathay a mere literal translation of his Chinese originals.) Two illustrations should suffice to give readers a flavour of his method.

The first example is from Fingal Book IV:

Chuir sinn Dio-ghrein suas re Crann
Bratach Fhein budh mor a treis
Lomlan do Chloichidh Oir
'S an linne gu ma mor a Meass.
Iomad Cloidheamh dorn Chran oir
Iomad Srol gu chuir re Crann
'N Cath Mhicumhail Fian na'm fleadh
'S budh lionar Sleagh os ar Ceann.

A literal translation would be:

We raised the Sun-beam on its pole -
the standard of Finn, great was his power.
Full it was of golden jewels,
and great we deemed its worth.
There was many a golden-hilted sword,
and many a banner raised,
in the battle of MacCumhail, the warrior of banquets,
and many were the spears raised above our heads.

Macpherson renders it thus:

We reared the sunbeam of battle; the standard of the king! Each hero exulted with joy, as, waving, it flew on the wind. It was studded with gold above, as the blue wide shell of the nightly sky. Each hero had his standard too; and each his gloomy men!

Macpherson appends a note: "Fingal's standard. To begin a battle is expressed, in old compostion, by lifting of the sunbeam."

His version conjures up the same image, but he darkens it with the gloomy men.

The next short example is from a sequel to Fingal, Temora. Most of this book is original Macpherson, and for that very reason, less well written, but he does have a Gaelic source for Book I:

Nuair chronnairc a Cairbre ruadh
Osgar a snaidhe an t sluaigh
An t-sleagh nimhe bha na Laimh
Go ndo leig e sin na chomhail.

Thuit Osgar air a ghlun deas
Sa n tsleagh nimhe roimh a chneas
Go n chuir e sleagh na naodh siong
Ma chumadh fhuilt agus eidin.

Literally:

When the red Cairbre saw Oscar cutting up the host, he hurled at him the poisoned spear which he had in his hand.

Oscar fell on his right knee, with the poisoned spear piercing his skin (but) he planted the spear of the nine rivets in the meeting of his hair and his face [ie forehead].

Macpherson turns this into:

Cairbar shrinks before Oscars' sword! He creeps in darkness behind a stone. He lifts the spear in secret, he pierces my Oscar's side! He falls forward on his shield, his knee sustains the chief. But still his spear is in his hand! See, gloomy Cairbar falls! The steel pierced his forehead, and divided his red hair behind.

Once again, Macpherson feels obliged to add the adjective "gloomy". Derick Thomson points out a flaw in Macpherson's understanding. He says that it is possible that Macpherson did not understand that sleagh nimhe = poisoned spear. And Thomson adds that "his knee sustains the chief" is a typical Macpherson rendering.

The Douai Manuscript

The Highland Society of London helpfully put together a lot of material about manuscripts of Ossian (see Bibliography). The quotations here come from that source or from letters sent to them.

On 12th February 1806, Bishop Cameron of Blackfriar's, Edinburgh wrote that he knew of a manuscript which seemed to be the originals from which Macpherson translated. He said it had been lost in France. A Rev. James Macgillivray, who went to Douai college in 1763 had seen the manuscript in the handwriting of John Farquharson, the Prefect of Studies at the college.

The Jesuit John Farquharson (1699-1782), who was born in Braemar, had "advanced to a high literary level from the lowly basis of Gairnside Gaelic". (Jesuits in the Highlands: Three Phases, by Alasdair Roberts, Journal of Jesuit Studies 7 (2020)) So, it is no surprise to see him preserving a collection of Gaelic literature.

Macgillivray and Farquharson felt that Macpherson's translation was not as good as the original (no surprise there). The manuscript contained more poems than had been translated by Macpherson and, in spite of Bishop Cameron's assertion, it is unlikely that he had seen this particular collection. But that it existed at all further refutes the claims of Doctor Johnson.

By 1775, the manuscript had fallen into disrepair and apparently some leaves had even been used to kindle a fire! (A manuscript of the Jesuit poet Gerard Manley Hopkins was said to have been used to kindle a fire at their college in Glasgow, so be careful where you lay your paperwork.)

Bishop Chisholm of Edinburgh wrote about it on 15th May 1806. He says that Farquharson wrote it out c 1745 (in other words, just before the suppression of Gaelic and other things

Highland) when he was a missionary in Strathglass, near Inverness. A Mrs Fraser of Culbokie had taught the Jesuit Gaelic.

James Macgillivray wrote on 10th May 1806 that whatever remained of the damaged MS "must have perished with everything else in that house [Douai college], during the French Revolution".

The Rev. Ronald Macdonald remarked to Bishop Cameron that Farquharson "seemed to think that similar and even fuller collections might still be formed with little trouble. He was not sensible of the rapid, the incredible, the total change, which had taken place in the Highlands of Scotland, in the course of a few years".

Mrs Fraser, it seems, also had a MS. Her son, Archibold, recollected that his brother Simon took their mother's MS with him when he emigrated to America in 1773. During the American War (1775-83), Simon was on the British side as an officer, was taken prisoner, and died in a dungeon. His sons, William and Angus, moved to Canada, but of Mrs Fraser's MS we hear no more.

John Farquharson talked about how he had made his "escape [from the French Revolution] in October 1793, at which point all British property became a national prey, and their first care would be to destroy all vouchers and documents". He goes on to say that "to contest the authenticity of the production [of Ossian], is giving the lie to a whole nation; yet what may we not expect from men determined not to believe, unless you show them, which is impossible, the very originals; the translator Macpherson has sufficiently warranted their unaccountable scepticism as to this point". Indeed, the "conduct of Macpherson, in suffering the least doubt or mystery to remain regarding the authenticity of Ossian, cannot possibly be justified".

David Hume (no less) "very justly condemns the absurd pride and caprice of Macpherson, who scorned, as he pretends, to satisfy any body that doubted his veracity".

"It has been ingeniously suggested, that Mr. Macpherson threw a mystery over the authenticity of Ossian, on purpose to make the works of that great poet more the subject of discussion, and it must be acknowledged, that his conduct, in some measure, had that effect."

The History Behind the Myth

But another question arises from all this: are these stories "mere" mythology or is there something historical behind them?

We are still finding out about the first few centuries of Scottish history. As I write this in 2020 an ancient Pictish hill town has just been unearthed about 45 miles inland from Aberdeen on the Tap O' Noth. There seems to have been about 800 huts for a population of about 4,000 people. This has been dated to the 3rd century CE which is possibly the period in which lived the man referred to in what is now Scotland as Fingal.

Cormac mac Art was said to be High King of Ireland c. 227-266 CE. During this period Finn Maccool was leader of his warrior band called The Fenians. So, if Finn/Fingal did exist, he lived c. 192-283 CE, too late to have known anyone at the time of Cuchullain.

In his The Decline and Fall of the Roman Empire, Edward Gibbon (1737-94, a contemporary of both Macpherson and Johnson) refers in a note on the subject of "the gospel among the tribes of Caledonia":

"Ossian, the son of Fingal, is *said* [original emphasis] to have disputed, in his extreme old age, with one of the foreign missionaries, and the dispute is still extant, in verse, and in the Erse [Irish Gaelic] language."

No gods, or indeed anything religious, is mentioned explicitly in Macpherson's Ossian (nor in Tolkien's Ossianic Lord of the Rings), although there are vague allusions to the Norse Gods from whom, of course, the British Isles still get the names of their days of the week. The Romans rather gave up on trying Scotland as a province, preferring the land south of the two walls. They did not even bother conquering Ireland. About 290 CE some Christian missionaries attempted to convert the inhabitants of this part of the world, but this is later than our tale of Fingal. A later myth says that the missionary Ossian was portrayed as having a dispute with was none other than Saint Patrick. More likely this story is about the reluctance of the people to give up their old gods.

After referring explicitly to Macpherson in a note to Ch XXV, Gibbon says this a few pages later:
"the *genuine history* [original emphasis] which he [Rev. Mr. Whitaker] produces of Fergus, the cousin of Ossian, who was transplanted (A.D. 320) from Ireland to Caledonia, is built on a conjectural supplement to the Erse [Irish] poetry, and the feeble evidence of Richard of Cirencester, a monk of the fourteenth century."

The following verse is from the Book of the Dean of Lismore:

"An Ughdar so Oiséan ...
Deiredh na Féine fuair nós
is me Oiséan mór mac Finn ..."
[The Author is Ossian ...
Last in line of the famous Fenians,
Is me, Ossian the great, son of Fingal]

So, did Finn/Fingal, his son the blind bard Ossian, his cousin Fergus, and the rest actually exist as historical characters? The simple answer is we simply do not know. But if they did, they probably came from Ireland, not what we now call Scotland, notwithstanding Macpherson wishing to think otherwise.

Swaran

Peter Frederik Suhm (1728-1798) published Historie af Danmark between 1782 and 1793. In it, he mentions Swaran, son of Starno. He also mentions the Irish hero Cuchullin and the Caledonian King Fingal. Apparently, Swaran was eventually killed by Gram who died in 240 CE which date fits neatly with the supposed timeline of Ossian and Fingal, but not really with the tales of Cuchullain.

Suhm has this to say:

"Swaran was the son of Starno; he had carried on many wars in Ireland, where he had vanquished most of the heroes that opposed him, except Cuchullin, who assisted by the Gaelic or Caledonian king, Fingal, in the present Scotland, not only defeated him, but even took him prisoner; but had the generosity to send him back again to his country."

Suhm goes on to say that after returning home to Jutland, Swaran had to engage in single combat with Gram whereupon Swaran lost his life: "he left sixteen brothers, seven born in wedlock, and nine by a concubine. These Gram was obliged to meet at once, and was fortunate to slay them all".

Suhm "places the death of Gram in the year 240, and from the context of the history, the transaction with Swaran cannot have happened many years before".

Thus Swaran, Starno, and Fingal (if not Cuchullain) would appear to be part of the genuine history of Denmark. Along with all students of history, we await further developments.

The Scots Musical Museum

It was Edinburgh's James Johnson, a printer, who conceived the idea of a collection of Scots Songs with music to be printed with pewter engraving rather than the more expensive copper engraving. He had already engaged the organist Stephen Clarke to transcribe the music when he met Clarke's friend, Robert Burns, then at the height of his fame. Burns enthusiastically took over the main editorial role from the end of Volume 1 which had already partly gone to press.

There are three songs which are "Ossianic" in the collection. In Volume 1 (1787) is a song with words by Miss Ann Keith and music by a Mrs Touch:

Oscar's Ghost

O see that form that faintly gleams!
'Tis Oscar come to chear my dreams;
On wings of wind he flys away;
O stay, my lovely Oscar, stay.

Wake Ossian, last of Fingal's line,
And mix thy tears and sighs with mine;
Awake the harp to doleful lays,
And sooth my soul with Oscar's praise.

The shell [drinking vessel] is ceas'd in Oscar's hall,
Since gloomy Kerber wrought his fall;
The Roe on Morven lightly bounds,
Nor hears the cry of Oscar's hounds.

In Volume 2 (1788), we get the genuine article, perhaps due to the influence of Burns. Robert Riddell says of The Maid of Selma:

"This air began to be admired at Edinr about the year 1770. The words are a little altered from the original in the Poems of

Ossian and I am doubtful whether the tune has any pretentions to antiquity."

But he later changes his mind:

"Since I wrote the above, I have met with a collection of Strathspeys &c. by John Bowie at Perth. In the end of the collection are three airs (said [to be]) by Fingal and the following note precedes them: - The following pieces of ancient music were furnished to the editors by a gentleman of note in the Highlands of Scotland, were composed originally for the Harp and which were handed down to him by his ancestors who learned them from the celebrated harper Rory Dall, who flourished in the Highlands in the reign of Queen Ann. This air there called The maid of Selma seems to be taken from these ancient Fingallian ones."

Rory Dall [dall = blind], The Blind Harper, is Ruaidhri Dall Mac Mhuirich aka Roderick Morison, c 1656 – 1714. Queen Anne, the last of the Stuarts, lived 1665 – 1714, and was Queen of England, Scotland, and Ireland 1702 – 1707 and then reigned as Queen of Great Britain and Ireland 1707 – 1714. In Volume 4 of The Scots Musical Museum (1792), a tune from Rory Dall was the original for Burns' Ae Fond Kiss.

The Maid of Selma

In the hall I lay in night, mine eyes half-clos'd with sleep,
Soft music came to mine ear
Soft music came to mine ear
It was the Maid of Selma.
Her breasts were white as the bosom of a Swan,
Trembling on swift rolling waves.
She rais'd the nightly song,
For she knew that my soul was a stream
that flow'd at pleasant sounds;
mix'd with the Harp arose her voice,
mix'd with the Harp arose her Voice,
She came on my troubled soul,

> Like a beam on the dark heaving ocean
> when it bursts from a cloud and brightens
> the foamy side of a wave;
> 'twas like the memory of joys that are past,
> pleasant and mournful to the soul,
> pleasant and mournful to the soul

The still sceptical Robert Riddell says of the next song: "Here is another Fingallian air – said to be…" To be accurate, all he means is that the tune does not seem to him to be ancient. There was a rumour that the tune came from Macpherson himself, but, as is normal with these things, there is no evidence to support that. The source of the words is The Songs of Selma: Colma.

Song of Selma

> It is night. I am alone, forlorn on the hill of Storms.
> The Wind is heard in the Mountain,
> the Torrent Shrieks down the Rocks,
> no Hut receives me from the Rain;
> forlorn on the Hill of Winds.
>
> Rise, Moon, from behind thy Clouds:
> Stars of the Night, appear! Lend me Light to the Place
> where my Love Rests from the Toil of the chace;
> His Bow near him unstrung, His Dogs Panting around him.
>
> But here I must sit alone, by the Rock of the mossy Stream;
> the stream and the wind Roar,
> nor can I Hear the voice of my Love,
> the voice of my Love.

Chronology of the Works of Ossian by Macpherson

1759	The Death of Oscar
1760	Fragments of Ancient Poetry
1761	Fingal ... with Several Other Poems
1763	Temora ... with Several Other Poems
1765	The Works of Ossian (2 vols.)
1773	New edition of Ossian

Epilogue

The Life of James Macpherson

Up to this point I have told you little of James Macpherson himself. Let us close by spending a few paragraphs looking at his life.

James Macpherson was born in 1736 in Badenoch. In a cave near that very place would hide for a short time none other than Prince Charles Edward Stuart. After the failure of the Jacobite uprising, the Highland way of life was under threat as was their very language. Prejudice against Gaelic was still strong for many years after the '45 rebellion. Fortunately for Gaelic, that was Macpherson's first language.

By 1758 he was working at Balfour publishers in Edinburgh. He published some original poems at this time – in English. One of these, The Highlander, is imbued with the heroic Gaelic tales of his youth and the defence of the land against Scandinavian invaders.

He began to publish his translations of actual Gaelic poetry in 1760 and made a collection of Gaelic originals. On 16th January 1761, he wrote to a Mr Maclagan: " I have been lucky enough to lay my hands on a pretty complete poem, and truly epic, concerning Fingal". He, and others, became convinced that these "fragments" were part of an actual epic and he edited the episodes together to produce Fingal. So popular was this book that more of the same was demanded from his adoring public. Unfortunately useable fragments ran out and so much of the later work is James Macpherson's own. Like many a sequel produced to respond to popular demand, this later work is neither as good as Fingal, nor as exciting to read. Despite this, many editions followed of the "works of Ossian".

James Macpherson's many influential friends included the British PM, Lord Bute. In 1764 Macpherson headed to

America as "secretary to the governor of the Western Provinces". He returned in 1766 to write propaganda for the government, histories of Great Britain, and a translation of The Iliad. India's Governor-General appointed him his agent in London. Macpherson by this time was making a lot of money. Thus he was able in 1780 to pay for a seat in the House of Commons. Nowadays, of course, buying one's way into parliament would (surely) not be tolerated.

He died in 1796 and his work was held in such high regard that he is buried in Poets' Corner at Westminster Abbey. In a final irony, he is buried beside the man who tried so hard to ruin his reputation, Doctor Johnson himself.

Bibliography

Blind Ossian's Fingal, Edited and Introduced by Allan Burnett & Linda Andersson Burnett, Luath Press Ltd, 2011

The Sublime Savage by Fiona Stafford, Edinburgh University Press, 1988

The Gaelic Sources of Macpherson's Ossian by Derick S. Thomson, 1952

The Poems of Ossian in the Original Gaelic with a literal translation into Latin by the late Robert MacFarlan, A.M. Together with a dissertation on the authenticity of the poems by Sir John Sinclair, Bart., The Highland Society of London, 1807

Poems of Ossian, Translated by James Macpherson, With an Introduction, Historical and Critical, by George Eyre-Todd, The Walter Scott Publishing Co., Ltd., 1912 (?)

The Poems of Ossian and Related Works, Edited by Howard Gaskill with an introduction by Fiona Stafford, Edinburgh University Press, 1996

The Reception of Ossian in Europe, Edited by Howard Gaskill, Continuum, 2004

The Scots Musical Museum 1787-1803 by James Johnson and Robert Burns, Scolar Press, 1991

Other Works by John McShane

Robert Burns in Edinburgh (with Jerry Brannigan & David Alexander)
How to Create Graphic Novels by Rodolphe Töpffer

Articles & Short Stories:

The Drouth
The Spirit 100th Anniversary
Comic Scene
Fantasy Advertiser
Amazing & Fantastic Tales
Jimmy the Zombie

As Publisher:

aka Magazine
The Bogie Man

Screenplays:

The Real Thing
Echoes